R0201353430

08/2020

W9-AKE-959

THE
SUMMER CAMP
FROM THE
BLACK LAGOON®

Get more monster-sized laughs from

The Black Lagoon®

THE
SUMMER CAMP
FROM THE
BLACK LAGOON®

by Mike Thaler
Illustrated by Jared Lee

SCHOLASTIC INC.

ABDO
Spotlight

In loving memory of Joe Belperio, the best Schneid of all —M.T.

To Skipper the dog —J.L.

ABDOPUBLISHING.COM

Reinforced library bound edition published in 2017 by Spotlight, a division of ABDO, PO Box 398166, Minneapolis, Minnesota 55439. Spotlight produces high-quality reinforced library bound editions for schools and libraries.
REPRINTED BY PERMISSION OF SCHOLASTIC INC.

Printed in the United States of America, North Mankato, Minnesota.
092016
012017

THIS BOOK CONTAINS RECYCLED MATERIALS

ISBN 978-0-545-55399-5

Text copyright © 2013 by Mike Thaler
Illustrations copyright © 2013 by Jared D. Lee Studio, Inc.

PUBLISHER'S CATALOGING-IN-PUBLICATION DATA

Names: Thaler, Mike, author. | Lee, Jared, illustrator.
Title: The summer camp from the Black Lagoon / writer: Mike Thaler ; illustrator : Jared Lee.
Description: Reinforced library bound edition. | Minneapolis, Minnesota : Spotlight, 2017.
 | Series: Black lagoon adventures ; #24
Summary: Hubie is being sent far away to summer camp and he can't even bring his TV or computer. Will he survive his vacation?
Identifiers: LCCN 2016953178 | ISBN 9781614796084 (lib. bdg.)
Subjects: LCSH: Summer--Juvenile fiction. | Camps--Juvenile fiction. | Vacation--Juvenile fiction. | Adventure and adventurers--Juvenile fiction.
Classification: DDC [Fic]--dc23
LC record available at https://lccn.loc.gov/2016953178

ANGRY FOX

Spotlight
A Division of ABDO
abdopublishing.com

CONTENTS

DISTURBED SNAKE

CHAPTER 1
EXILE

Mom doesn't love me anymore. She's sending me away.

She's shipping me off to summer camp for seven days.

I've never been away from home for more than seven hours.

I've never missed a dinner, or spent a night out of my own bed.

← MOM

CAMP

I'll have to eat there.
I'll have to sleep there.
I'll be all *alone*.
Mom isn't coming with me.

CHAPTER 2
BUMMER CAMP

Mom shows me the camp brochure.

There's a picture of a big lake . . . the one I'll drown in.

There's a picture of a big
forest . . . the one I'll get lost in.

There's a picture of a big
mountain . . . the one I'll fall off
of.

Mom says it looks beautiful.

If it looks so beautiful, why doesn't she go and let me stay home?

CHAPTER 3
CALL OF THE WILD

I'm desperate. I call Eric for sympathy.

He's happy. He's going to baseball camp. They get to play baseball all day.

They get caps and uniforms. I wish I could go there.

FANTASTIC VIEW →

ASSISTANT COACH ↓

I call Derek. He's happy, too. He's going to tennis camp. They get to play tennis all day.

He'll have a ball. What a racket!

GOOD SHOT!

Randy's going to soccer camp.
That'll be a lot of kicks.

Freddy's going to cooking camp. All he's taking is a knife, fork, and spoon.

16

Penny and Doris are going to ballet camp. That should keep them on their toes.

I'm going to a wilderness camp.
My only sport will be *survival*.

And with all my friends away, I
won't know anybody, and nobody
will know me.

I'VE NEVER SEEN YOU BEFORE.

I'M FROM PAGE 34.

CHAPTER 4
PACKIN' IT IN

Mom says we should start packing. She has a list from the brochure. We have to take a first-aid kit (oh, great!), a flashlight, warm socks, a backpack, and a sleeping bag.

The list says we have to sew my name into all my clothes. That's so they can identify the body.

I want to take my video games, my computer, the TV, all my baseball cards, and my entire closet. Mom says they're not on the list. But I can take my pillow.

Now that we're done packing, Mom says I should go to bed because we have to get up very early. Don't most executions take place at dawn?

21

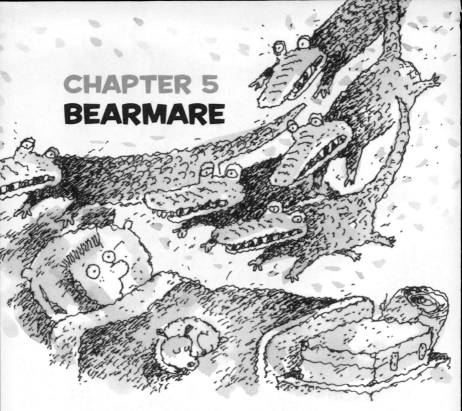

I can't sleep. I try to count sheep. But instead I count bears, mountain lions, wolves, skunks, coyotes, snakes, spiders, scorpions, mosquitoes, bats, and alligators. Finally I do fall asleep and have a dream.

It's "Hubie and the Three Bears."

Mom has sent me to the deep, dark woods to pick berries. I get lost. There are no street signs or streetlights. Suddenly, I see a light between the trees. It's a little cabin just like the ones at camp. I go in. There are three bowls of porridge on a wooden table. I'm hungry. I eat them all. Then I see three beds. I'm tired. I lie down and fall asleep.

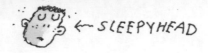

Suddenly, I'm woken up by a hairy paw shaking me. There are three bears standing over me.

"It's Goldilocks," says the baby bear.

"That's not Goldilocks," says the mamma bear, reading the label sewn on my shirt, "it's *Hubie*."

"Let's eat him," says the poppa bear.

The alarm goes off. Saved by the bell. I open my eyes, but it's still dark outside.

"Rise and shine!" chirps my mom from the other room.

I hate camp already.

CHAPTER 6
THE EARLY WORMS

I sit numb in the car as the sun tries to climb out of the night.

Finally, we pull into a parking lot. There are lots of moms shoving unhappy kids onto a purple bus that says *Camp Sherwood.*

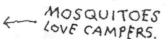

← MOSQUITOES LOVE CAMPERS.

I *Sherwood* like to go home. Mom kisses me on the forehead, hands me my backpack, and marches me onto the bus.

It's full of sleepy kids with morning mouth.

Some are crying. Some have quietly accepted their fate.

I'm still hoping for a pardon from the governor.

I sit down next to the biggest kid.

"What's your name?" I ask.

He looks at the label sewn inside his shirt.

"Jerry," he says.

I look at my label.

"I'm Hubie," I say.

STRAINING HIS NECK →

We shake hands.

"You know any camp songs?" he asks.

"No," I answer, "but I know a knock-knock joke. Knock-knock."

"Who's there?"

"Sherwood."

"Sherwood who?"

"I *Sherwood* like to go home."

"Me, too," he says, and smiles.

CHAPTER 7
BUSTED

The driver closes the door and starts up the engine.

The moms all wave good-bye as we pull away.

"I think this vacation is for them," says Jerry, looking out the window.

GOOD-BYE.

SO LONG.

WE'LL MISS YOU.

All signs of civilization slowly disappear.

No more buildings, billboards, street signs, fast-food restaurants, stoplights, streetlights, or neon lights.

It's a good thing we have our flashlights.

HEADED TO THE UNKNOWN

HERE COMES FRESH MEAT.

Jerry asks the bus driver if he knows any camp songs.

He says he knows one, and starts to sing "Ninety-nine Bottles of Root Beer on the Wall."

By the tenth time through we all know the words, and by the twentieth time we're driving under an old wood sign that says, *Welcome to Camp Sherwood: Home of the Bears.*

SAW

CHAPTER 8
BUZZ OFF

We all pile out of the bus and line up. I stay close to Jerry.

I look around—we're in the middle of eight little cabins, just like the ones in my dream. Maybe this *is* a dream. Maybe I'll wake up.

A guy blows a whistle.

"Welcome to Camp Sherwood," he says. "My name is Buzz."

I wonder if his last name is *Saw*. He's big. He has one eye. We find out later he lost his other eye last summer. I wonder what he'll lose this summer. . . .

"I'm the camp safety director and your counselor," he says.

He blows his whistle again.

"Pick up your gear and follow me."

I don't have any gear . . . I'm on automatic.

CHAPTER 9
HIGH AND DRY

Buzz leads us to one of the cabins.

"Go pick a bunk and meet me at the mess hall."

"Why do they call it a *mess hall*?" I whisper to Jerry.

"You'll find out," he says, "and be sure to get a top bunk."

"Why?" I ask as we hurry in.

"Bed wetters," he says, while climbing up to a top bunk.

I grab the last one.

MY NAME IS HUBIE.

I WANTED TOP BUNK.

37

CHAPTER 10
OUT TO LUNCH

We all march into the mess hall and sit down. I still don't know why they call it a mess hall.

Then they bring out the food and I figure it out.

BON APPÉTIT.

HOLD YOUR NOSE.

FOOD

Echh . . . it's a mess! Mashed everything.

Mashed potatoes, mashed peas, squashed squash.

The chef must be King Kong.

This makes the school cafeteria look like a four-star restaurant. Well, the good thing is you don't have to cut anything . . . or even chew it.

DON'T SQUASH MY BONE.

After lunch it's time to go swimming. I hope we wait at least a half hour so we don't drown.

40

CHAPTER 11
FOR GOODNESS' SNAKES!

We march back to our cabin and put on our bathing suits. Then we walk barefoot down to the lake.

There are all sorts of sharp, prickly things on the ground.

"Ouch!" "Ouch!" "Ouch!"

Pine needles, pine cones, sticks and stones that can break your

bones. I walk carefully.

We get to the lake and it looks cold. Maybe we should go ice skating instead.

"Jump in, boys," shouts Buzz, and he blows his whistle.

We just stand there. I raise my hand.

"I'd like to know a little about the aquatic life before I leap in," I say. "For instance, are there any snapping turtles, piranhas, or sharks?"

"No sharks." Buzz smiles. "But look out for the snakes."

"Snakes! No way, I'm not going in there."

Buzz winks his good eye, "In ten years, I've only seen one."

"Yeah, well that one won't see me." I sit down on a log. "Ouch!"

This log has just as many sharp places as the ground. Uncomfortable!

All the kids are splashing around. Looks like they're having fun. There are snakes in logs, too. Maybe I'll take my chances in the water.

CHAPTER 12
IN THE SWIM

Wow! Swimming is cool. I can swim down to the bottom and open my eyes. It's got a lot more stuff in it than a swimming pool.

There are plants, and rocks, and little fish. It's sorta like an aquarium. Jerry and I play sunken pirate ship and look for treasure.

47

Jerry finds an empty soda can, and I find a rubber sandal.

When Buzz blows his whistle, no one wants to get out.

We're having too much fun. But it's time to go canoeing.

I've never been in a boat before. I hope I don't get seasick.

CHAPTER 13
WHAT'S CANOE WITH YOU?

We all line up and Buzz gives us each a life preserver and a paddle.

Then he assigns us a canoe, two by two.

Jerry and I are shipmates, and we climb in.

"Whoa!"

It's like getting into a hammock. We both finally flop down in seats. I'm in the back, so I have to steer. But there's no steering wheel. Buzz shows us how to steer with our paddles.

Cool.

Jerry and I decide to paddle along the shore. That way, if we sink, we can walk home. Hey, some kids are going out to the center of the lake. I wonder what's out there.

It's boring along the shore, so we paddle out after them. Soon we're in the middle of the lake. It's like being in the center of the world, or outer space. The sun sparkles on the water like stars. We can't even see the shore.

53

I bet it's deep out here. At least a hundred miles down.

Other kids paddle by and splash us with their paddles.

"Let's get them back."

We paddle fast and catch them. Soon we're in the middle of a great sea paddle battle!

I'm Sir Francis Drake, and they're the Spanish Armada.

We would have won, but Buzz blows his whistle and we have to come in.

Tomorrow we'll have another great battle, but for now, let's just dry off.

CHAPTER 14
YAY, CAMP SHERWOOD

That afternoon, we make lanyards, see a woodpecker, and play volleyball.

For dinner, we build a campfire. Buzz shows us how to start a fire without matches. He says you can use a magnifying glass to focus the sun's rays. This doesn't work too well at night. Jerry wants to try it with his glasses and the moon. Bummer.

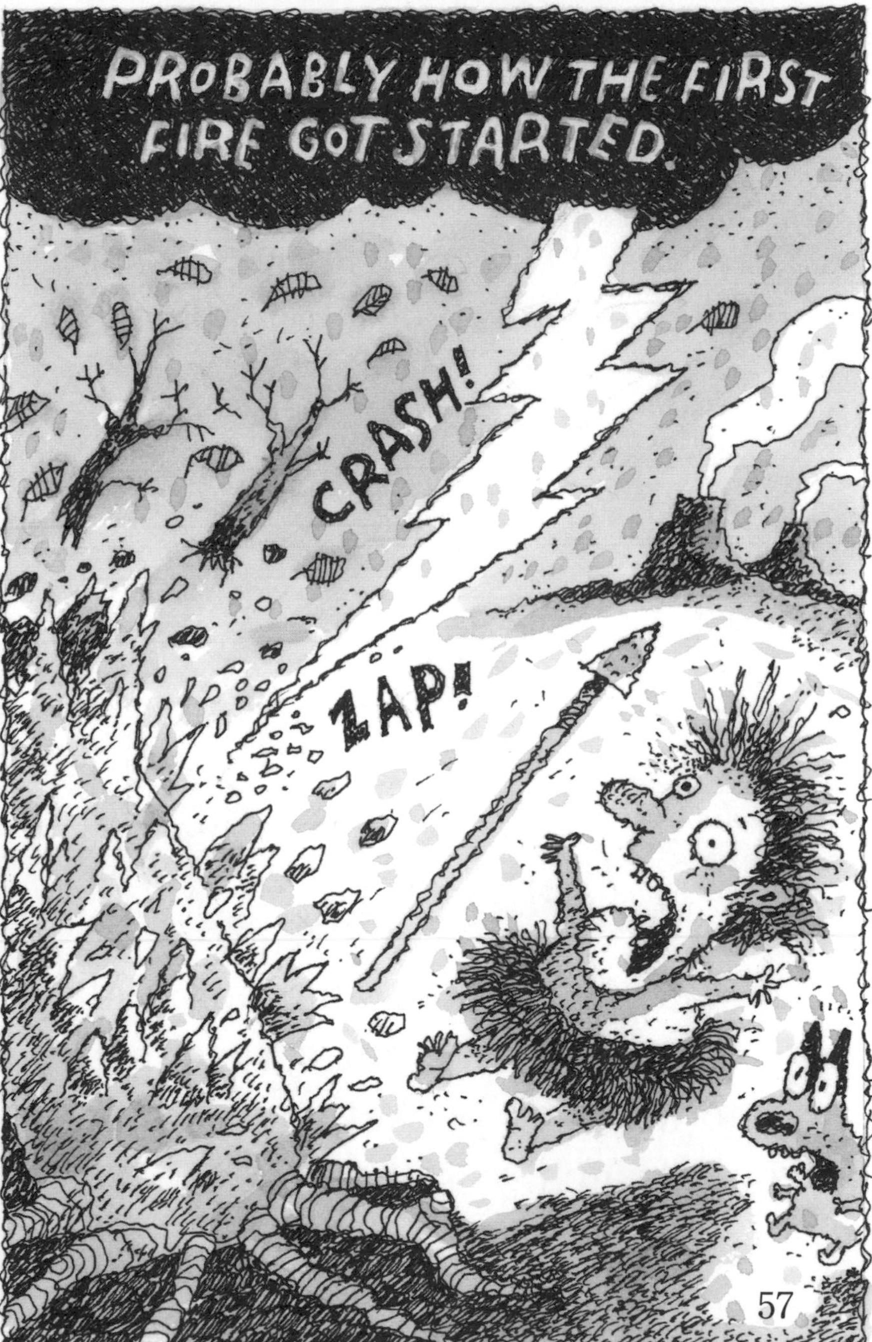
PROBABLY HOW THE FIRST FIRE GOT STARTED.
CRASH!
ZAP!

Instead, you can strike a piece of flint on a stone.

Also, you can spin a stick so fast on leaves that the friction starts a fire.

FASTER.

"But that takes an hour and I'm hungry," says Buzz, reaching into his back pocket and pulling out a match.

Soon we have a roaring fire and are roasting hot dogs and marshmallows on sticks. Jerry and I put a marshmallow at each end of a hot dog and call it a *marshdog*. Soon all the kids are making marshdogs and we're heroes.

After dinner, we all sit around the campfire singing, and then when it gets really dark, Buzz tells us a ghost story.

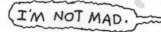
I'M NOT MAD.

CHAPTER 15
PLAYING CHICKEN

The ghost story is about a mad scientist who takes a living chicken heart and gives it vitamins.

Thump, thump ...
It grows bigger ...
Thump, thump ...
And bigger ...
Until it fills up the whole laboratory.
Thump, thump.

CHICKEN WITH A HEART

Then it eats the scientist, which really makes him mad, and the chicken heart thumps out into the night looking for another snack.
Thump, thump!

Then Buzz puts his flashlight under his chin and clicks it on.

"And now . . . it's here!" he shouts.

When all of our hearts stop thumping, we walk back to our cabins under the stars.

I climb into my bunk. I don't want to go to sleep. I don't want this day to end. I don't want this week to end. I wish I could stay at camp longer.

As I close my eyes, I hear the night. I hear all the creatures that are lucky enough to be at camp all summer.

And I think I can even hear the stars.